THE FENCE

A Mexican Tale

Story and pictures by Jan Balet

A Seymour Lawrence Book
Delacorte Press / New York

Mexico is a land of volcanoes
and tropical forests, of snow
and fierce heat, of meadows
and deserts, of cities and
villages, of big dogs and
little dogs, and, like every-
where else in the world, of
rich people and poor people.

In Mexico, once upon a time, there was a very rich family who lived in a beautiful pink house with a huge green garden. Often rich people look well fed and happy, but the people in the pink house looked glum and miserable. Even their dog and their parrot were skinny and bad-tempered, although the house and the kitchen were full of everything one could desire.

Next door to the pink house
lived a poor family. Their
house was a little thatched
hut. Between the two
houses stood a big fence.
Sometimes poor people are
tired and unhappy, but not
this family. The children
glowed with health, although
their house and kitchen were
small and almost bare. They
always made the best of
what there was. Even their
guinea-fowl and their cat
looked happy. The sound of
their children's laughter
could often be heard through
the fence and this annoyed
the rich people next door.

In the rich family's kitchen people were always busy, roasting, boiling, baking, and frying. All day long glorious smells drifted through the fence. Early in the morning came the smell of hot chocolate. At noon it was the mouth-watering aroma of roast meat. And in the evening every breeze brought a smell of chicken or grilled fish or sometimes even of spicy duck. No wonder the mother of the poor family would hand each of her children a slice of bread and say, "Now go and stand by the fence, and smell something good to enjoy with your bread."

One day the father of the
rich family got very angry
when he saw the children
of the poor family standing
by the fence and sniffing.
"Go away, you gang of
thieves!" he yelled at them.
"I'll send you to jail for
stealing the smell of our
food." And sure enough,
on the next market day,
the poor family and the rich
family were called by the
judge to appear in court.

On their way to court, both families stopped at the village market. Tradesmen from other villages had spread out their wares all over the market place. The lady from the pink house arrived with her cook to do the shopping. She was very fussy and haggled over everything: hair ribbons, baskets of eggs, tropical fruit from the south, hens, fried pancakes, and flowers.

All around her were stalls
piled high with fruit: oranges,
lemons, melons, bananas,
and grapefruit. There were
also loaves of bread made
in all shapes and sizes, and
still warm from the oven.
Dogs barked. Old ladies
gossiped. Everyone sniffed
the glorious smell of the
new-baked bread, but none
of the bakers complained.

The family from the little
thatched hut usually enjoyed
market days. They liked the
crowds, the excitement, the
music, and the jokes about
the bullfight. They laughed
at the people in masks and
tried to guess who they
were. But on this particular
day they were sad. No
one likes to have to
appear in court even if
he is sure he is right.

The trial was to begin at
eleven o'clock. The rich
family arrived early
and was very elegantly
dressed. The poor family
arrived late, in their
everyday clothes. Their
children looked down at
the ground because
they were frightened.
Still, they hoped that
their father would be
able to settle everything.

The judge called for silence and then told the rich man to speak first. The man from the pink house described how he paid his servants to cook the most delicious meals. But, he said, this did not help his family at all, because the wretched family next door stood by the fence and sniffed all the goodness away from the food. "Look how well fed and happy they are!" he said. "That proves I am right."

The judge thought about this for a long time. Then he asked the father of the poor family what he had to say. "May I leave the room for a moment?" the poor man asked. Standing just outside the door, he put a few coins into his sombrero and shook them so that they jingled loudly. His family began to laugh as he slyly asked the rich man whether he had heard the clink of the money. The rich man nodded. The judge understood what the poor man meant and gave them his decision. "You," he said to the rich man, "have heard the jingle of this man's money, just as he sniffed the smell of your food. If he owed you anything for the smell, he has paid you back."

The poor family was delighted.
They rushed home and held
a fireworks party to
celebrate their victory—
for in Mexico if people
are happy they always let
off rockets. They did not
make anyone pay to watch
the rockets or to listen to
them, and they let the
wonderful smell of the burnt
gunpowder drift across
the fence—absolutely free.